Franklin Says I Love You

To Bob and Robin, for the love we share — B.C.

Franklin is a trademark of Kids Can Press Ltd.

Text © 2002 Contextx Inc.
Illustrations © 2002 Brenda Clark Illustrator Inc.

Interior illustrations prepared with the assistance of Shelley Southern.

Kids Can Press acknowledges the financial support of the Ontario Arts Council,
the Canada Council for the Arts and the Government of Canada, through the
BPIDP, for our publishing activity.

Kids Can Press Ltd.
29 Birch Avenue
Toronto, ON M4V 1E2

www.kidscanpress.com

Edited by Tara Walker

Printed in Hong Kong by Wing King Tong Company Limited

CM 02 0 9 8 7 6 5 4 3 2 1
CDN PA 02 0 9 8 7 6 5 4 3 2 1

National Library of Canada Cataloguing in Publication Data

Bourgeois, Paulette
    Franklin says I love you

ISBN 1-55337-035-X (bound)   ISBN 1-55337-034-1 (pbk.)

I. Clark, Brenda II. Title.

PS8553.O85477F886 2002   jC813'.54   C2001-902228-X

PZ7.B6654Fxs 2002

Kids Can Press is a Nelvana company

Franklin Says I Love You

Written by Paulette Bourgeois
Illustrated by Brenda Clark

Kids Can Press

FRANKLIN thought he was very lucky. He thought
he had the best pet goldfish. He thought he had
the best friends and the best stuffed dog. But, most
of all, Franklin thought he had the best mother in
the whole wide world.

Franklin's mother baked fly pie, just for him.

Franklin's mother played catch, even when she was busy.

And Franklin's mother always read him two stories before bed, even when she was tired.

So when Granny told Franklin that his mother's birthday was the very next day, he decided to give her the best present ever.

Franklin wanted to show his mother how much he loved her.

Every year, Franklin made a birthday present for his mother.

She had loved her macaroni necklace.

She had hung Franklin's self-portrait on the wall.

She had even worn her birthday hat shopping.

This year, Franklin decided to buy his mother something fancy.

He emptied his piggy bank and went to town.

Franklin looked in all the stores.

But everything cost too much.

"How can I show my mother I love her," he wondered, "without a fancy present?"

So Franklin went looking for help.

He walked along the path and over the bridge until he came to Bear's house.

"Bear," said Franklin, "how can I show my mother I love her without a fancy present?"

"I always make my mother breakfast in bed," said Bear.

But Franklin's mother had told him that she didn't like crumbs in bed.

Franklin walked through the berry patch until he came to Snail's house.

"Snail," said Franklin, "how can I show my mother I love her without a fancy present?"

"I always bring my mother flowers," said Snail.

But Franklin had given his mother a bouquet of dandelions just the day before.

Franklin walked across the meadow until he came to Beaver's house.

"Beaver," said Franklin, "how can I show my mother I love her without a fancy present?"

"I always draw my mother a picture with hearts and flowers and X's and O's."

"X's and O's?" asked Franklin.

"Kisses and hugs," explained Beaver.

But Franklin always hugged his mother when he came home from school, and he kissed her every night.

Franklin walked around the pond until he came to Goose's house.

"Goose," said Franklin, "how can I show my mother I love her without a fancy present?"

"I always make my mother some pretty jewelry," said Goose.

But Franklin's mother already had a macaroni necklace and a string of pearls.

Franklin was tired and hungry.
He walked all the way home.
His mother's birthday was the next morning,
and Franklin still didn't have a present.

Franklin asked his father, "How can I show Mother that I love her without a fancy present?"

"You do nice things for her every day," answered Franklin's father. "Why do you ask?"

"Because tomorrow is her birthday," said Franklin.

His father looked surprised.

"Why don't you and your sister make her a card?" he suggested. "I'll run to the store."

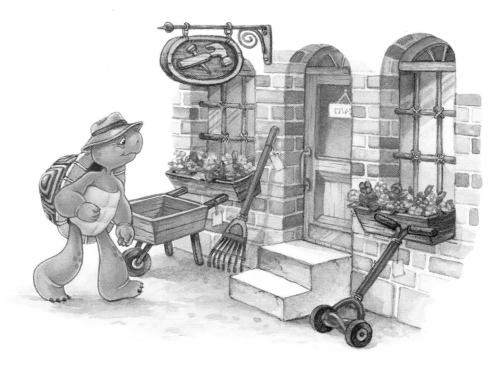

Franklin helped Harriet make a card, but he did most of the work.

Sometimes he wished he was little like Harriet. She never worried about anything.

Early the next morning, Franklin had an idea.
He would do *everything* his friends suggested.
  He made his mother a pretty brooch.
  He drew her a picture with double X's and O's.
  He cut fresh flowers from her garden.
  And he put her breakfast on a tray.
  Franklin tried his very best.

Franklin and Harriet sang "Happy Birthday" to their mother.

Then she ate her breakfast in bed and brushed away the crumbs.

She pinned her brooch on her pajamas.

She said she loved Harriet's card, Franklin's picture and the tool kit from Franklin's father.

"You've made this a wonderful day," said Franklin's mother.

But Franklin wasn't finished giving presents. He had planned one more thing — something he'd thought of all by himself.

Franklin gave his mother a hug and a kiss, and then he said, "I love you."

"Those three little words are better than any fancy present," said Franklin's mother.

Right then, Franklin knew he'd found the best way of all to show his mother he loved her.